To Camelia Garrison —

Best Wishes!

Robert Lutz

5/16/06

Grandma's Biscuits

By Robert Little
Illustrated by Jamea Richmond

RELDE Publishing

DEDICATION

I dedicate this book to the memory of my mother, Lula B. Little—the greatest biscuit maker ever.
— R.L.

I would like to thank my family and friends who have supported me throughout the years.
— J.R.

Little, Robert, 1959-
    Grandma's biscuits / by Robert Little; illustrated
  by Jamea Richmond.
    p. cm.
    SUMMARY: A little boy loves his grandma's
biscuits--and his grandma.
    Audience: Ages 3-7
    ISBN 0-9701863-5-5

    1. Grandmothers—Juvenille fiction. 2. Grandparent
and child--Juvenile fiction [1. Grandmothers--Fiction.
2. Grandparent and child--Fiction. 3. Biscuits--
Fiction.} I. Richmond, Jamea. II. Title.

    PZ7.L72526Gra 2004   [E]
              QB133-1751

Library of Congress Control Number: 2004091252

For additional books and to contact Robert Little
for speaking engagements:
RELDE Publishing, LLC
P.O. Box 21304, Jackson, MS 39289
www.reldepublishing.com
www.robertlittlespeaker.com
1-800-489-3439

I love Grandma's biscuits as I watch them grow. When I'm waiting to eat them, time passes so slow.

I love Grandma's biscuits one, two or three. Grandma made these biscuits just for me.

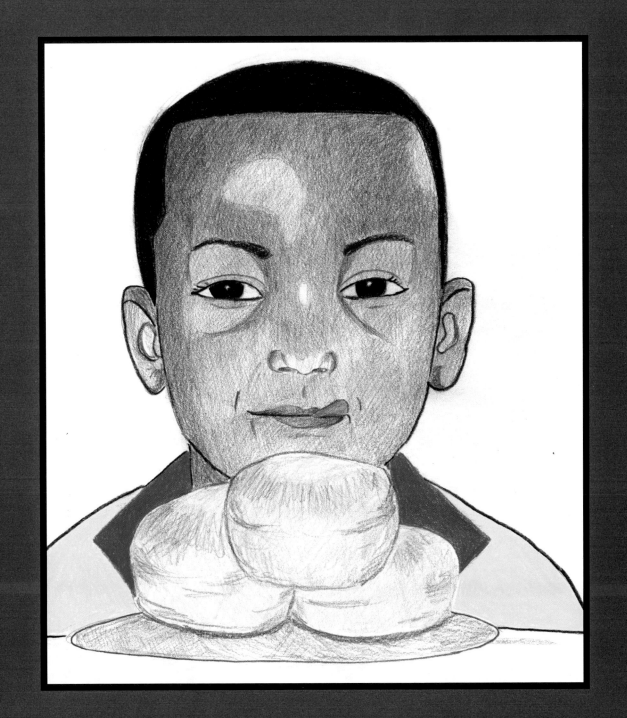

I love Grandma's biscuits
with a drumstick.
I eat to grow strong,
so I'll never be sick.

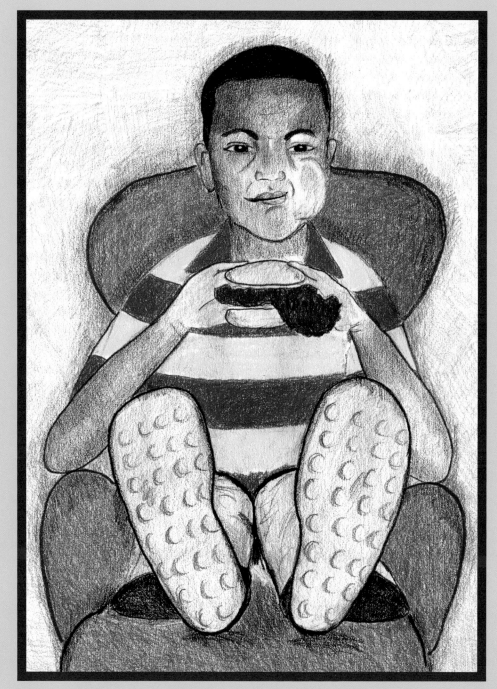

I love Grandma's biscuits
with a big, green pickle.
They sell them at the store
for a dollar and a nickel.

I love Grandma's biscuits
with ice cream.
My friends snack with me
as we beam.

I love Grandma's biscuits
with spaghetti this way.
I eat my sandwich fast so
that I can play.

I love Grandma's biscuits
while kicking a ball.
I'm very, very careful so
that I don't fall.

I love Grandma's biscuits
as I swing high in the
sky.
Grandma's biscuits are
better than candy, pizza
or pie.

I love Grandma's biscuits while riding my bike for fun. Grandma's biscuits help me jump, kick and run.

I love Grandma's biscuits while doing math. After I'm done, I take a good, hot bath.

I love Grandma's biscuits while in the tub. Why everyday? Once a week is plenty to scrub.

I love Grandma's biscuits while dreaming about what I can be. A teacher, doctor or lawyer—just wait, you'll see!

I love Grandma's biscuits
in the morning and at
night.
After eating them,
I know the bedbugs
won't bite.

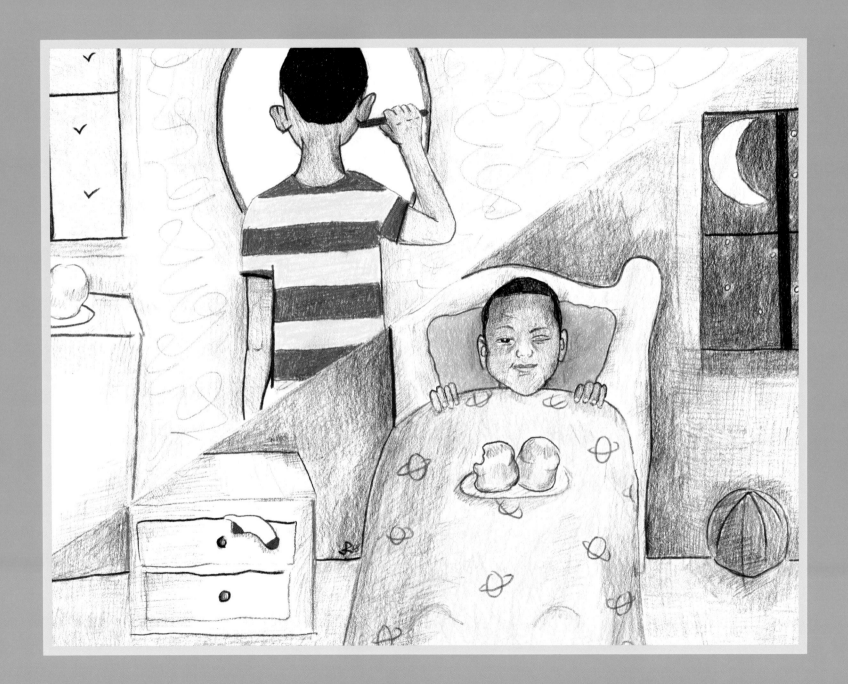

I love Grandma's biscuits—watching as she sings and bakes. Once the biscuits are done, maybe she'll make cakes.

But, most of all, I love Grandma's biscuits with Grandma.